THE GRUFFALO

◆ A special book for WORLD BOOK DAY ◆

based on THE GRUFFALO
by Julia Donaldson and Axel Scheffler

MACMILLAN CHILDREN'S BOOKS

He has terrible tusks

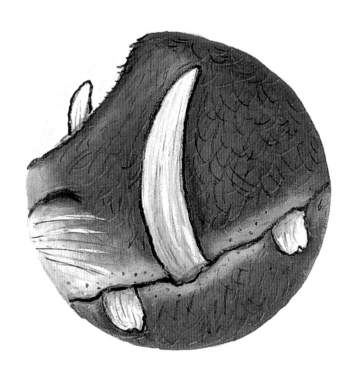

And terrible claws

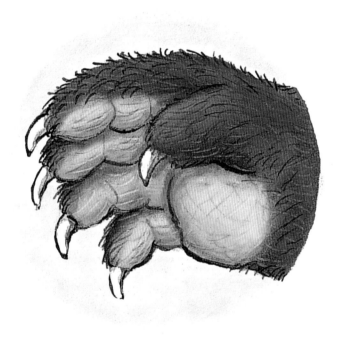

And terrible teeth
in his terrible jaws.

He's the Gruffalo, Gruffalo, Gruffalo.
He's the Gruffalo!

He has knobbly knees

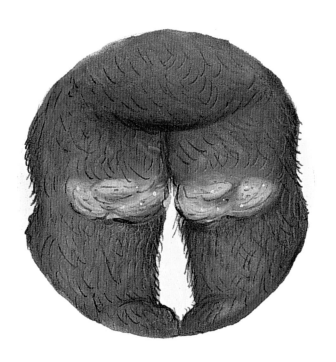

And turned-out toes

And a poisonous wart
at the end of his nose.

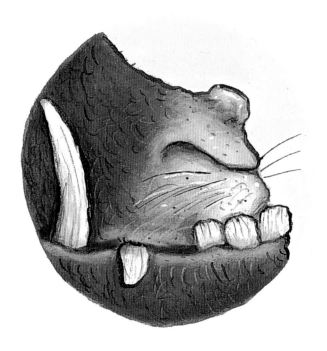

He's the Gruffalo, Gruffalo, Gruffalo.
He's the Gruffalo!

His eyes are orange.

His tongue is black.

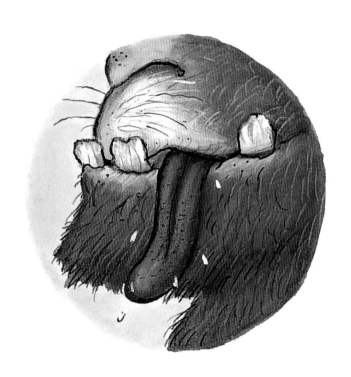

He has purple prickles
all over his back.

He's the Gruffalo, Gruffalo, Gruffalo.

He's the Gruffalo, Gruffalo, Gruffalo.

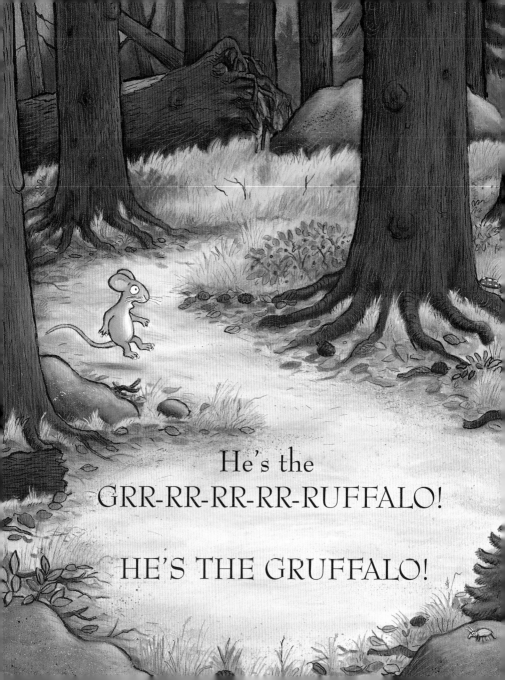

He's the
GRR-RR-RR-RR-RUFFALO!

HE'S THE GRUFFALO!

Here's the tune to the Gruffalo song, so you can sing along!

THE GRUFFALO

JULIA DONALDSON